After Charlotte's Mom Died

Cornelia Spelman

Illustrations by Judith Friedman

Albert Whitman & Company • Morton Grove, Illinois

For my own: Sam and Kate. C.S.

For Jacquelyn Murphy Beresford, with many thanks. J.F.

Library of Congress Cataloging-in-Publication Data

Spelman, Cornelia.
After Charlotte's mom died / written by Cornelia Spelman;
illustrated by Judith Friedman.
p. cm.
Summary: Because her mom's death causes six-year-old Charlotte to feel sad, mad, and
scared, she and her dad visit a therapist who helps them acknowledge and express their feelings.
ISBN 0-8075-0196-4
[1. Death—Fiction. 2. Fathers and daughters—Fiction.]
I. Friedman, Judith, 1945– ill. II. Title.
PZ7.S74727Af 1996
[E]—dc20
95-38320
CIP
AC

The text typeface is Bembo.
The illustration media are watercolor and colored pencil.
The design is by Karen A. Yops.

AUTHOR'S NOTE

When a child's parent dies, we feel helpless, but actually we can help a lot. We can help by allowing a child to feel the deep sadness that such a death brings, by sitting close, by holding a hand or embracing, by crying together. This sharing of pain makes it bearable.

Of course we wish to protect a child from this pain, so we often try to deny it. However, we need to resist the impulse to divert attention from a loss, to minimize, or to give false reassurance. Usually when we try to cheer someone up, it's because we can't tolerate the feelings aroused in us by that person's sadness. Yet, just accepting what another person feels without trying to change it can be immensely comforting.

Close listening is important because it will reveal a child's misconceptions and fears about death. Often these are ideas that might not occur to adults, but can torment a child. A child also needs to know that despite the loss of a parent, there are still family members or friends who love and will continue to care for her or him.

Perhaps most important, a child needs to feel hope. While the precious person who died will always be missed, the child will not always feel such an enveloping sadness. Time will bring new adventures, new satisfactions, new people to love. A child most needs to know that happiness will continue to be possible, and was not buried with the dead.

Cornelia Spelman, L.C.S.W., A.C.S.W.

Charlotte was six years old and lived with her dad and her favorite stuffed animal, Godfrey. Charlotte lived just with her dad and not with her mom because her mom was dead. She had died in a car accident when Charlotte was five and a half.

Since Mom died, Charlotte's dad had been very sad. Sometimes he cried. He seemed busy a lot, and he often didn't seem to hear or see Charlotte.

Sometimes Charlotte cried, too. Other times she felt angry. Why did her mom die? Why didn't she come back so Charlotte could see her, and so her dad wouldn't have to be sad?

At night, Charlotte was afraid to fall asleep. Aunt Gloria had told her that being dead was like being asleep. Too, Charlotte thought about what would happen to her if her dad died. Then Charlotte would be an orphan and have to go live in an orphanage.

Charlotte had a lot of thoughts like this, and she only told them to Godfrey.

On the outside, Charlotte looked like she used to, when her mom was alive. She went to school and took her bath, just like before. On the inside, though, Charlotte felt different. She felt sad and mad and scared. She felt like she had lost something very precious, and would never find it again.

One day when the girls at school were playing
house, Charlotte said she'd play the mom. A girl named
Joanie said, "You can't! You don't have a mom, so you
can't play it!"

Charlotte's mixed-up feelings whirled around inside
her like a storm.

"I do TOO have a mom!" she yelled, and before
she knew it, she had pushed Joanie so hard that Joanie
fell and hurt her arm.

Charlotte's dad had to come to school to talk to the teacher. Charlotte felt sad and mad and scared as Dad and the teacher talked.

When Dad was finished talking, instead of being mad like Charlotte thought he'd be, he used his softest voice, the one Charlotte had hardly heard since Mom died. Dad put his arms around Charlotte and said, "I guess I didn't realize how upset you've been because I've been too busy being sad about Mom's death.

"I decided you and I will go see someone who can help us with our feelings so we can be happier. This someone is called a 'therapist,' and her name is Anna."

Charlotte liked Anna's office. It was full of things to play with, and Anna didn't say, "Don't touch that!" like Aunt Gloria did. Also, Anna had a cat named Tiger who was orange and white with big, soft paws.

There were stuffed clowns in Anna's office, and Charlotte liked to play the "family game" with them. Once she had the mother clown have a car accident, just like what had really happened to her mom.

Another time Charlotte pulled the hat on the father clown down over its face and ears. "He can't hear or see the little clown," Charlotte explained to Anna. "The little clown had a bad dream, and her daddy didn't listen."

One day, Charlotte showed how the little clown
was afraid to go to sleep because Aunt Gloria had said
being dead was like being asleep.

Charlotte's dad was with her in the office. When he
heard this, he cried. "I didn't know that, Charlotte," he
said. Anna always held Dad's hand when he cried, and
never said, "Now cheer up and give me a big smile!"

Anna told Charlotte that people sometimes said
being dead was like being asleep, but that wasn't really
correct. It was safe for Charlotte to go to sleep, and it
would not make her dead.

Anna told Charlotte that she needed to tell her worries to her dad and not just to Godfrey. So Charlotte told Dad about being afraid she'd be an orphan.

Dad said, "I don't think anything's going to happen to me. But there will always be someone in our family to love you and take care of you, and you will never have to go to an orphanage."

Uncle Joe, Aunt Carmen, and Charlotte's favorite cousin, Georgie, told her, too, when she and her dad went there for dinner. "We'd take care of you," Georgie said.

Charlotte needed to cry, and Georgie held her hand until she was done. "Let's eat cake!" said Georgie when Charlotte was finished crying.

Anna had a beautiful pink stone that Charlotte could pick up and hold. Anna told her it was a special kind of wishing stone. "If you say the wish out loud, we can see if we can make it come true, or if it's the kind of wish that can't come true," said Anna.

Charlotte held the smooth pink stone in her hands. "I wish," she said, closing her eyes, "I wish that my mom wouldn't be dead anymore."

"Oh," said Anna, "I know you and Dad both wish that, and so do I. But that's the kind of wish that can't come true, and so you both feel very, very sad."

Anna said, "Let's think of a wish that *can* come true." She held the stone in her own hands. "I wish," she said, closing her eyes, "that Charlotte and her dad can be happy again even though Mom is dead."

Charlotte and her dad looked at each other. Dad reached out his arms to Charlotte, and they cried and cried. Charlotte let out all those feelings that were like a storm inside her. As Dad held her, she felt like she was finding something precious, even if it wasn't the something she had lost. Maybe everything could be right again.

Anna said, "As time goes on, those happy feelings will get bigger and bigger, and those sad feelings will get smaller and smaller."

Suddenly Charlotte's dad laughed and pointed to Tiger. Charlotte saw that Tiger had curled up with Godfrey and was licking his face. Charlotte laughed, too. It felt good.